Be a Hero.
Be a Friend!
Sue Fitz

The HERO in ME

Written by
Susan Fitzsimonds

Illustrated by
Jeff Covieo

Ferne Press

The Hero in Me
Copyright © 2012 by Susan Fitzsimonds
Illustrations by Jeff Covieo
Illustrations created with digital graphics
Layout and cover design by Katheryn Hansen
Printed in the United States of America

Summary: A young boy decides to stand up for what is right and to teach others.

Library of Congress Cataloging-in-Publication Data
Fitzsimonds, Susan
The Hero in Me /Susan Fitzsimonds–First Edition
ISBN-13: 978-1-933916-94-1
1. Juvenile fiction. 2. Standing up for others. 3. Bystanders. 4. Making good choices. 5. Bullying. 6. Self-esteem.
7. Responsible behavior.
I. Fitzsimonds, Susan II. Title
Library of Congress Control Number: 2012931220

FERNE PRESS

Ferne Press is an imprint of Nelson Publishing & Marketing
366 Welch Road, Northville, MI 48167
www.nelsonpublishingandmarketing.com
(248) 735-0418

To my three favorite "heroes," Peyton, Keira, and Leah,
Mommy loves you very much.

To anyone who has stood up to a bully, your courage is heroic.

I'd like to thank Nelson Publishing & Marketing for their dedication to this project. Thanks to Marian Nelson and Kris Yankee for their hard work, support, and encouragement throughout this process.

Thanks to Jeff Covieo for bringing the text to life with incredible illustrations.

I'd like to thank all of my students for opening up to me and sharing what it feels like to be a kid in today's world.

I'd like to extend a special thank you to my parents for being an amazing source of love and support throughout my entire life. They are an example of a good work ethic, unconditional love, and, above all, faith in God. I am blessed to have such great role models in my life.

Most of all, I would like to express my appreciation to my husband, Chris. Thank you for being an outstanding source of support and for teaching me never to take life too seriously. Your sense of humor brightens up my life! I love you.

There's a hero in me. It's not hard to find.
I have to listen to my heart, soul, and mind.
Each day of my life I have choices to make.
These choices decide which road I will take.
One road is positive; it makes me feel proud.
The other is not; I just follow the crowd.

It's not always easy. In fact it's quite hard
to do the right thing, never let down my guard.
I need to be thoughtful, patient, and kind,
help people out when they get in a bind.
I'm sure to face struggles each passing day.
That's fine 'cause I solve them the "hero in me" way.

One time at recess, we started to play,
but one chose to act like a bully that day.
His words were hurtful; his temper was flaring.
I knew I would have to say something quite daring.
Then the hero in me came out with a roar.
I said, "You can't play here like that anymore."

It's scary to speak up when someone is yelling,
but heroes show confidence, and that's very telling.
Stand tall, speak up, and make your voice heard.
The bully must hear your every last word.
Tell them to stop it; be very specific.
You'll be surprised; it feels quite terrific.

The next day I noticed my best friend was sad,
so I stopped and asked her what was so bad.
She told me a bully was riding her bus,
name calling, pushing, and causing a fuss.
The hero in me knew how to react;
kind words will have a lasting impact.

When you notice someone is feeling upset,
the best thing to do is to help them forget.
Offer a compliment, invite them to play,
give them a smile and brighten their day.
That's when you'll know that a friendship is real.
They look out for you and care how you feel.

On the third day this bully was at it again.
He called me a loser and then stole my friends.
I wanted to hit him square in the eye
and tell him that he was a terrible guy.
But the hero in me said that just wasn't right,
because nobody wins when you choose to fight.

When someone at school calls me a name,
I want to yell back and treat them the same.
That's when I step out and breathe really deep,
think happy thoughts, or even count sheep.
Then I feel calm; I've passed this test.
A hero will try to do what is best.

On the fourth day this bully was rip-roaring mad,
'cause when bullies don't win, they act really bad.
We all tried to keep our distance outside.
If he's on the swings, we'd play on the slide.
The bully just followed us every which way,
and the hero in me didn't know what to say.

I knew it was time to ask for some help.
I had to report this, couldn't fix it myself.
Right after school, I told an adult.
She let me know this wasn't my fault.
She promised to help, even taught me some tricks,
said there is no problem too big to fix.

Here are some things that my teacher taught me.
It all fits together like a great recipe.
Believe in yourself, stand tall on your feet,
even when bullies try to turn up the heat.
Then speak your mind; say "stop it," "we're through."
His words may seem hurtful, but they are untrue.

But sometimes you tell an adult, and then
the bully continues again and again.
So if this happens, do not dismay.
Go tell them again and do not delay.
When you say nothing, adults think that it's done,
and you are left thinking that your bully won.

If you're feeling courageous, here's what you should say,
"Why do you do these things day after day?"

I'll bet you the bully has no real reason
for all of his put-downs, anger, and teasin'.
He might be surprised you decided to ask.
His true self is hiding in his bully mask.

Another day at recess, to my surprise,
this bully said, "Hey, can I play with you guys?"
Part of me wanted to say, "No way,"
but I remembered that's not what a hero would say.
I thought to myself, it must be my turn
to lead this bully and help him to learn.

But this bully needed to find some new ways
to handle his temper when it was ablaze.
I could teach him, but that's not enough,
because learning new things can be really tough.
I told him to find an adult he could trust
and ask them for help on how to adjust.

As we talked to each other, we started to see,
I was like him, and he was like me.
We both enjoyed pizza, soccer, and games.
We knew it's not right to call people names.
I really liked him when he wasn't mad.
I realized that no one is really all bad.

While I explained to this bully about how he should be,
there's also a lot he was teaching me.
Like sometimes you need to give people a break,
find out why they're making the choices they make.
We never know all the hurts they may feel.
Their lives may have problems that need time to heal.

On the last day we all made a new rule:
we must act like heroes at home and at school.
Heroes take turns. They listen and share.
When playing a game, they make sure that it's fair.
If we make good choices about how we should play,
we're certain to have a much better day.

SHARE

PLAY FAIR

TAKE TURNS

LISTEN

But if we are bothered by one acting so rude,
we won't let them play with that attitude.
Instead we might say, if you're gonna stay near,
we have a rule that you need to hear.
Heroes are welcome; no bullies allowed.
You must be kind to be part of this crowd.

If you're with friends on the playground at school,
and you witness someone who is just acting cruel,
it is your job to offer assistance.
Heroes show loyalty, love, and persistence.
My true friends like me just how I am.
They speak up for me when I get in a jam.

When kids get bullied and adults are not there,
we must do more than just stopping to stare.
You may be surprised, but kids hold the power
to end all this meanness, this very hour.
Your teacher and parents can show you the way,
but it's up to heroes to end this today.

I'm glad that I found this hero in me.
I've decided it's who I will always be.
Some days it's easy and others it's not.
I'm not always perfect. I practice a lot.
It takes hard work, but that's okay.
It all pays off at the end of the day.

So now you know about the hero in me.
Look at yourself. What do you see?
You have some really big choices to make.
Who will you be? Which road will you take?
I have a job I'd like you to do,
it's time to tell about the hero in you!

A Hero's Guide to Reporting a Bully

⇨ You don't want to sound like you are tattling, so do not rush up to the teacher after lunch or recess or when they are very busy and blurt out your problem.

⇨ Go to your teacher or another trusted adult and say, "I have a problem. When is a good time for me to talk to you?"

⇨ When you have the adult's undivided attention, tell them what is going on and be sure to tell them all the things you have already tried on your own to get rid of the bully.

⇨ Wait a week or so to see what happens.

⇨ If nothing changes, many children assume that talking to the teacher or adult did not help. If the adult does not hear from you again, they may think that the problem is fixed.

⇨ Go back to the same adult and say that your bully is still bothering you (as many times as you need to). This way they will know whatever they did is not working and something more needs to be done.

A Hero's Guide to Standing Strong

Confidence is a skill. It can be taught and must be practiced. Role-play using your confident voice, wording, and body language with your family or pet, or even by yourself in front of the mirror.

Have good posture–Stand tall, head up, and look that bully right in the eyes.

Use a confident voice–Speak firmly and loudly enough to be heard without yelling.

Address others by name–Confident people address others by their names. If you want to really stand up to someone, say their name before you tell them to stop. *Ex.: "Joey, stop calling me a loser."*

Be specific–Confident people say exactly what they need. You cannot tell your bully to stop being mean, annoying, or a bully. People who act that way usually don't get it if you say that. You need to say the exact behavior you want them to stop. *Ex.: "Anna, stop pushing me out of line." "Sam, stop repeating everything I say."*

Be careful–Even if the bully has really hurt your feelings, respond with confidence and a "who cares" attitude. You'll have a better chance of making it stop if you don't let them know they have hurt you.

Don't be mean back–Confident people do not need to put others down to make themselves feel good. Even if you want to call them a name right back or even push or hit them back, you are a hero. You know that true strength is shown through positive choices.

Don't ever say please to a bully–Remember you are not asking them to do you a favor. You are using confidence to get them to treat you with respect. This does not require please or thank you.

20 Things a Hero Might Say to a Bully

"Whatever."

"So what."

"Oh boy, here we go again. Do you feel better now?"

"Why do you care so much about me?"

"Don't waste your breath."

"Does it make you feel good to be this mean?"

"Don't you have anything better to do than bug me?"

"Your opinion doesn't matter to me."

"I don't really care what you think."

"Why do you do this?"

"[Name], stop calling me a [whatever they called you]."

"You really need to stop [whatever it is that is bothering you]."

"Get a life, and quit bugging me."

"Maybe you didn't get the memo—I don't care."

"Maybe you didn't get it the first time—stop calling me a [name]."

"I'm sorry you feel that way. I don't agree."

"Keep talking if you want. I'm not listening."

"I will never feel bad because of your words. Give up."

"Wow, you're funny."

"I'm sorry, were you talking to me?"

A Hero's Tips for Good Friendships

Be yourself–You should not feel like you have to act differently around certain people. A true friend will not try to change you. Just remember to treat others the same way, and do not tease others for their differences.

Apologize and forgive–Everyone makes mistakes. When you do something wrong, just admit it and say you are sorry. When your friend does something wrong, forgive them and move on.

Allow your friends to have other friends–Don't be a friend hog. People do not like it when you tell them who they can and can't be friends with. Your friends will like you a lot more if you let them play with other people sometimes. That does not mean that they don't like you anymore, so don't worry.

Be a good sport–No one likes to play with a poor sport. If you are winning a game, don't rub it in your opponent's face. And if you are losing, don't quit.

Show respect–No name calling, gossiping, or spreading rumors. If someone begins to talk about a friend who is not there, change the subject or leave the conversation.

Be careful what you say–Never tease people about things they cannot control or their personal preferences. These might include physical appearance, religion, gender, ethnicity, or family makeup (Yo Mama jokes seem funny until you make them about someone whose mother has passed away or just left them). Kids cannot control how much money their parents make, so they have no say in the type of house they live in or where they buy clothes. Don't tease others because of where they shop.

Susan Fitzsimonds began her career as an educator eleven years ago as a second grade teacher. During this time, she pursued her master's in counseling from Oakland University. She obtained a K–12 counseling endorsement, a counseling license, and specialization in child and adolescent therapy. She is currently in her eighth year as an elementary counselor working with children in kindergarten through sixth grade. Susan has also facilitated Love and Logic parenting courses and led presentations on the topics of bullying, cyber-bullying, self-esteem, and parenting. She has a passion for helping children increase their self-esteem, overcome adversity, and learn skills for dealing with difficult situations. Susan lives in southeast Michigan with her husband, three children, and miniature Schnauzer. Between church, family, and work, Susan has a very active life. For more information about Susan, please visit her website, www.susanfitzbooks.com.

Jeff Covieo has been drawing since he could hold a pencil and hasn't stopped since. He has a BFA in photography from the Center for Creative Studies in Michigan and works in the commercial photography field, though drawing and illustration have been his avocation for years. Other titles illustrated by Jeff include *Cuddling Is Like Chocolate*, *Read to Me, Daddy! My First Football Book*, *Kyle and Kendra Go To Kindergarten*, *Logan and Lilly Go To Kindergarten*, and *The Ride of Your Life: Fighting Cancer with Attitude*.